Hooky Cooky Ollie

By Gary Murrell

Illustrated by Madhu Greet

These stories are dedicated to the following:
Alice (Alms), Holly (Hols), Harry, Evie,
Lexie, Jacob, the children of the Priors School
in Warwickshire and, of course, Ollie the
working cocker spaniel.

Ollie's Snarl Off

"**D**angerous dogs. Nasty dogs! You'll have to be very careful, young man. I see that there are some untamed hounds on the moor. There can be no more motor cycling up there with Uncle Beage until they're caught," muttered Grandpa Basset in his west country drawl.

"Hooky cooky," said Ollie as he often did in a moment of amazement, excitement or even horror. This was bad news to Ollie as he was itching to get over to see his uncle in Tavistock Wood.

Grandpa Basset's favourite room was the kitchen and Ollie loved it too. It was strewn with the comforts of an old hound's life and smelt of liquorice, crusty paws and the muddier side of the countryside. The open fire flickered magically on a cold day, while Grandpa sat in his mahogany chair chewing his favourite sweets. Coconut fragments laced his soft, wet nose and his lips were black and shiny with liquorice. Sweet boxes and wrappers littered the floor and burst from half opened, dusty cupboards. To Ollie, a slightly grubby and scraggy black working cocker spaniel this was a wonderful world.

Sundays were when Gramps, as spaniel Ollie liked to call him, pawed over the washed and worn pine table scrutinising the local newspaper for news while the younger dog stood on a stool and peered over the basset hound's shoulder waiting expectantly for an announcement.

Gramps squinted at the 'Dartmoor Doogle' once more through his magnifying glass, his whiskers twitching, then suddenly turned to face Ollie nose to nose. Gramps' weak and chocolate brown eyes stared at him through his wire framed spectacles for some many moments until he spoke.

"These hounds have been chasing sheep and growling at hikers," said Gramps as he withdrew to his chair, popping a peppermint liquorice whirl into his mouth as he settled.

"Double hooky cooks," whistled Olls, as he was known to his family and best friends. His eyes were now as large as saucers, his nostrils as wide as ten pence pieces. He jumped off the stool, his tail in perpetual motion like an aeroplane propeller as he followed Gramps to the fire and sat beside its warm glow. Olls loved to consume its heat from the stone floor but he could not settle today while his mind was buzzing with the prospect of danger and adventure and possibly disappointment too.

Olls knew that the Baskerville family had difficulty controlling their hunting dogs ever since they had attached them to extendable leads but this was unacceptable and more importantly would put an end to explorations of the moor on Uncle Beage's prized but slightly oily motorbike. Something had to be done and quickly!

There was no time to lose so Olls left Gramps drifting

into sleep by the fireside, his spectacles slipping from his coconut covered snout.

Olls' heart pounded and his ears flapped like a blackbird's wings as he sped through the garden gate and across the muddy ploughed fields. He was one of the fastest runners ever seen in these parts, which Gaz said was because of his pedigree. His father was a Welsh field champion with a very long and difficult name to pronounce but otherwise known as Pop Ricks to the pups.

Meeting up with Uncle Beage at Tavistock crossroads was always keenly anticipated but today was doubly exciting given the danger of the dogs on the moor. He was late and he could already hear the throaty buzz of Uncle's motorbike before he could see it.

"Late today, my young man. Something kept you?" barked the beagle gently while passing a black riding helmet to Olls.

"Been reading the 'Dartmoor Doogle' with Gramps who said that I couldn't go to the moor with you while the vicious hounds were on the loose. They're a menace and a danger and probably bullies but we could sort them, couldn't we uncle........?" The spaniel was now out of breath and his pink tongue lolled from his mouth.

"Yes, heard about them too and Grandpa is right about that. Always put safety first. They were loose

again last night, chasing chickens and a farmer and foxes too. They must be avoided."

"So let's get onto the moor and teach them a lesson about bullying and.........."

"Best let the Dartmoor dog wardens deal with them. We'll have to go across to safer pastures today, young man, possibly pay a call on your Aunt Agatha instead over by Misperton Meadow. You haven't visited your aunt since you were last here on holiday. I am sure she'd love to see you and she hasn't been too well herself. Won't that be nice?"

As the motorbike's engine drummed into life and they accelerated down the wintery lane, Ollie felt dismal and his mood became as gloomy as the deepening grey skies above. He clung tightly to Uncle Beage's waist. No adventure on the moor was disappointing enough but visiting Aunt Agatha made matters worse. Ollie had never known laughter or fun from her and she kept a long and dismal face beside her black, flat ears. No one could begin to imagine her breed and there were never any treats (tweats as Olls called them), no liquorice either, just a dry biscuit for tea and long tortuous stories of her childhood during the war. And why was she known as 'Aunt'? She was clearly no relation to Uncle Beage.

Dismounting from the motorbike a few minutes later, Olls wished he was back with Gramps Basset snoozing by the fire. Uncle Beage led the way to Agatha's front

8

door in his leather biking jacket which was slightly too small for him these days. They had both removed their helmets and held them tightly by studded straps in their paws. Oll's tail curled beneath him, a sure sign of displeasure. Perhaps she would be asleep and not hear them knock, he hoped.

He was to be disappointed once more.

Aunt Agatha's sad eyes and whiskered snout soon appeared from behind the cottage door. She was wearing a black lacy bonnet which almost covered her eyes and made her look more miserable than ever, thought Olls.

"Oh, it's you two," she grumbled showing several stained and brown front teeth, one of which was badly chipped and others that were slightly loose.

"Did you say you were calling today? I am quite forgetful these days. Anyway, what do you want?"

"Just dropped by to see that you're well, Agatha. A surprise visit really, while Ollie is staying with Grandpa Basset for a few days. There are some dangerous dogs loose on the moor, you know and anyway Ollie was keen to see you and hoped that you might have some of those delicious biscuits for tea. Isn't that right, young man?"

Olls said nothing but just nodded, his eyes fixed to the doorstep while avoiding her curious breath and scrutinising a spider which was scuttling across the mat.

Aunt Agatha said nothing, just snorted then turned on her tail and crept back into her cottage which seemed so small and insignificant, planted as it was, in the corner of the field at the edge of a larger estate. Uncle Beage then Olls reluctantly followed her. The front room smelt of musty damp and stale biscuits. There were large pieces of fluff and crumbs on her fireside rag rug and from the ceiling a cobwebbed covered lampshade shielded a yellowing light bulb.

Uncle Beage suggested that he made them a bowl of tea each which he and Aunt Agatha settled down on the threadbare rug to sip. Olls was offered water and one of Aunt's biscuits and sat on the floor raising his eyes to watch more spiders abseiling from their webs.

"Did I tell you how about my evacuation here during the war, child?" Aunt Agatha looked up from her bowl and directly at Olls. She called all children or dogs younger than herself, 'child'.

Both Uncle Beage and Olls said in unison, "Yes, you have......very interesting too."

"There was rationing, of course, and we had to queue for coal and there were no treats for children or dogs and the Winter of 1947, just after the war, was bitterly cold. Our paws were frozen. The family on the estate treated me well but then of course........." Aunt Agatha only paused to catch her breath and slurp more tea from her bowl.

Both Uncle Beage and Olls had heard Aunt Agatha's reminiscences at length and on several occasions before but this did not deter her delight in enthusiastically retelling them again and again in even greater detail each time.

"Well, of course, you can see from the photo on the mantelpiece that I was a stunning young dog after the war. Beautiful, I was told by a number of local young hounds and one poodle in particular. Of course, I still don't have a grey hair in my fur to this day. Not bad for an old girl, eh?"

Olls looked down from the webs and scrutinised her greying muzzle. He did not fancy eating the biscuit.

"Anyway, then of course, in 1942........." Aunt Agatha had hunched her shoulders and fixed her gaze on Uncle Beage who appeared too frozen by it to move. She was enjoying the next instalment of her story which gave Olls the opportunity to slink away into the small passageway. Olls was good at slinking away unnoticed when he tried.

But what can be done about those vicious hounds on the moor? Nothing while I am trapped here with Aunt Agatha, Olls thought. Nose to the ground the spaniel sniffed his way around the rest of the cottage inquisitively, hoping to find more insects to inspect or anything which would capture his interest or be the start of an adventure. Occasionally, he shook his head, chewed a dead fly or sneezed as dust and assorted debris tickled his nostrils. From the front room he could still hear the constant drone of Aunt Agatha's voice.

About five minutes and several sneezes later Olls came across an object which caught his attention. In the corner of the passageway was an old pine box. More promising thought Olls. By wedging his snout under the rim of the lid he found that he was soon able to push it up to rest against the back wall. So dim was the light that Olls could not clearly see the contents of the box but that did not matter. Spaniels have an acute sense of smell and he was soon able to inspect the lumps and bumps of the box and the clothes by rummaging his head through the tangle.

"Hooky cooky," whistled Olls through his teeth.

"Of course, it was always felt by the Fulham Stage School in my younger days that I should have a career in the theatre but then the war came and evacuation." The voice continued from the next room which on this occasion was no bad thing. It gave Olls longer to investigate the box.

Soon he had pulled out an assortment of items which lay scattered on the floor and a black cloak with a maroon lining had now draped itself over him. There were peacock feathers, a magician's wand, a ventriloquist's dummy, a pair of false teeth, giant spectacles, a can of glow in the dark fluorescent paint, some hairy claws, several wigs, one which was particularly black and curly, and much more that Olls could not identify.

For some inexplicable reason he had an irresistible urge to gather up as many of the items as he could into his mouth and show them proudly to Uncle Beage and Aunt Agatha while wagging his tail vigorously. He often felt this inclination to show and tell when either excited or particularly pleased with himself. Sometimes this desire confused or even embarrassed Olls himself but Gaz had told him that it was nothing

to be worried about. It was part of being a retrieving dog, apparently.

Scooping what he could into his soft jaws, Olls trotted back to the main room.

14

"Well, I always thought the jive to be my best dance but others said that my waltz would become the talk of the West End…." Aunt Agatha was now in full swing and gesticulating with her paws. She was not even discouraged by the fact that Uncle Beage's head was resting on his chest. His beagle eyes drooped heavily while little snorting snores could be detected. He had clearly fallen asleep.

He was awoken only when Olls dropped his gifts onto the rug in front of Aunt Agatha who stopped recounting her memories and yelped, "Where did you find those, child?"

She fixed the spaniel with a stare as Uncle Beage coughed and spluttered back into life.

Olls avoided her gaze and instead looked down at his collection. He remained draped in the cloak.

"Well?"

"I found them in a box outside this room and thought they might be special treasures," Olls said sheepishly as the cloak slipped from his shoulders and onto the floor.

Aunt Agatha looked neither angry nor displeased. "I don't think they are worth anything. Just some odd bits left lying around the place and other pieces thrown in there by your Grandpa Basset from his younger days. He loved amateur dramatics and would always be part of the local talent show in the village hall……oh and he hosted fancy dress parties too at Christmas."

Uncle Beage stretched and yawned. "Well, time for us to be getting back, young man. Grandpa will be expecting you and the light is beginning to fade. We don't want to be any later with those hounds on the loose. I'll drop you outside Grandpa's house."

"You can take those things on the floor back with you, child. Most probably belong to your Grandpa, anyway."

The late afternoon light was dim and grainy grey by the time they set off. Aunt Agatha's eyes peering beneath her bonnet at the window as they mounted the Triumph troubled Olls a little. Should he have taken more interest in his elderly and clearly quite lonely aunt he pondered. Next time, perhaps.

Gramps Bassett was standing by the door of his stone and timbered house wrapped in a tartan shawl and leaning on a stick when Uncle Beage dropped Olls off a few minutes later.

"Called in to see Aunt Agatha this afternoon, Grandpa. Talkative as ever. Kept well away from the moor, though. Any more news on those vicious Baskerville hounds?" Inquired Uncle Beage as he dismounted. The air was cool and steam puffed from his mouth and nostrils as he spoke.

Grandpa said little in reply but just shook his heavy jowls instead.

"Don't forget those bits and pieces from your Aunts," said Uncle Beage simultaneously turning to Olls and fumbling with the straps which had held a green canvas bag to the back of the motor bike during their return journey.

Within a few moments Olls had hugged and licked Uncle Beage goodbye and momentarily watched his back disappear into the gloom and exhaust fumes before trotting towards the house, canvas bag hanging from his mouth.

Dinner was always served promptly at 6pm on the kitchen table and today was no different. Gramps Bassett had recently become enthralled by cookery programmes on 'Channel k Nine' television and was keen to treat Olls to his latest gravy or "jus" as he referred to it now. "Dartmoor Dazzler" was tonight's culinary creation, a very crusty meat pie which dripped slowly in a brown liquorice jus. It was not the most appetising of meals but Olls preferred it to yesterday's sausage and black pudding whirl encased in peppermint and coconut jus.

"More jus, Ollie?" questioned Gramps looking up from his own bowl while brushing fragments of crusty pie from his lips with the back of his paw.

"So tasty but so, so, so full, Gramps." Gramps had not quite mastered the correct consistency for jus, yet. Nevertheless, being particularly hungry the spaniel slurped the last of the meal from his bowl including the carrots which were his favourite vegetable and very healthy as they helped a dog see in the dark.

"Early to basket, tonight, Olls," said Gramps from his end

17

of the table. "Gaz will be here first thing in the morning for your journey back to Northamptonshire. Don't want you tired ....remember to brush your canines before bedtime....... and oh, take that bag upstairs with you too. What's in there? Not more of your Aunt Agatha's stage souvenirs, I hope."

The elderly hound had hardly finished his words before Olls had galloped to the top of the stairs and then into his bedroom to re-examine the 'souvenirs' from Aunt Agatha's.

Olls snuffled in the bag and pulled out the cloak followed by the teeth. He swung the cloak over his shoulders and slotted the plastic teeth into his jaws. They were Christmas cracker gnashers and felt uncomfortably enormous as did the hairy claws which were now on his paws.

"Errrrrrrr.......'orrible!" Olls leapt back from his bedroom mirror. "Double hooky cooks!"

He had shocked himself to the point of shivering. His reflection was of the scariest and hairiest creature he had ever seen or heard about! Slowly he raised his head once more to the mirror. Is this me, he thought? He eyes were wide dark pools which made him look even more terrifying. Olls was a kind and soft soul and had never imagined that he could be frightening. For fun he had once wanted to audition for a part as a ferocious wolf in the adventure film 'Dangerous Dogs' alongside famous actors but was too gentle to pass his elementary growling tests.

However, within a few moments an idea had occurred to Olls. He opened his jaws to reveal fangs and snarled. Scary, really, really, very scary! Without the fangs he could snarl in a friendly sort of way, if he chose, and in the summertime played a competitive game in the garden with Gaz called 'Snarl Off'. This is where both he and Gaz put their chins to the lawn and bottoms in the air while facing each other in a menacing way, revealed their teeth and snarled until one or the other was frightened away.

But this was different. This was to be a proper encounter. The Baskerville hounds were bullies and dangerous and would be challenged to a serious snarl off until so terrified by his outfit that they would return home and learn their lesson! He hoped. They could not be allowed to frighten people and animals from the moor, concluded Olls.

Olls knew that Gramps would never allow him to leave the house at night with or without dangerous hounds on the loose so he would have to wait. And wait Olls did in his basket covered in a blanket to disguise his costume. Gramps appeared in his striped gown and night cap before 7 O'clock and brought him his bedtime liquorice biscuit before disappearing to his own basket on the next landing.

"Sleep tight, Ollie," yawned Gramps as he shut the door behind him.

Olls must have fallen asleep at least twice before he heard the grandgramps clock in the kitchen strike 11pm. This was his time even though he was worried of gramps hearing him and absolutely petrified of the hounds.

Stealthily, he crept out of his basket and passed his mirror not daring to glance at himself even in the half light. With his working cocker speed and limitless stamina it would not take Olls long to reach the edge of the moor.

Half an hour later Olls was there, his paws sweating and aching inside his costume claws after a strenuous climb up the hill. Drifting in the breeze a few strands of broken bracken had caught on the base of his cloak and pulled at any undergrowth. The night was crisp and dark and smelled of wet fur with only brief glimpses of moonlight peering from the broken clouds to light his way. He was too scared to venture deeper into the moor for fear of becoming lost but there was no sight or sound of any hounds.

There was instead silence yet a sense of nocturnal movement all around him. What should he do? Just wait until caught in an ambush by the slashing jaws of evil hounds or become chilled to death while waiting for them? Gramps could wake at any moment and discover him missing from his basket. That would mean another type of trouble for him. Energetically his tail wagged but in fear not joy.

Suddenly, a frightened rabbit ran from beneath a bush

and scurried in front of his twitching nose. A panting Olls held his paws together and prayed: "Please keep me safe from harm, particularly from ferocious hounds with enormously sharp teeth, dear Lord....I promise to listen patiently and smile through all Aunt Agatha's long stories and enjoy all of Grandpa's jus, even the liquorice, fish paste, turnip and mushroom one....and....."

Before he could complete his prayers there was a sound of crashing and crunching bracken surrounding him and horrifying howls followed by the sight of deep and dark moonlit eyes. It was the Baskerville hounds! There were three, possibly four.

Olls sprang up into the night in terror. His false costume claws stretched high above his head and reached into the sky while his cloak, caught by the beasts' billowing breath, widened like a vampire's. He appeared at least three times his normal size. The spaniel's mouth opened wide to reveal vicious fangs glowing fluorescently. He had sprayed them from the paint can from Aunt Agatha's box before retiring to his basket.

"This is a snarl off! Do your worst!" He growled like some American gangster pretending to feel bold and making himself appear as large as possible as he landed then bounced on his hind feet into the air once more.

The enemy, lined up in front, snarled too. They were enormous. Baring his teeth once more, Olls stretched his cloak while gouging the air between himself and the hounds with his enormous party claws.

It was his last effort before closing his eyes in exhaustion and fearing the very worst! This was to be his valiant end.

There was the briefest of silences before the unmistakable sound of large padded feet running away across rough ground was all Olls could hear. Cowardly squealing and yapping followed moments later.

Then there was nothing.

Next only Ollie's gentle panting, his own tiny puffs of steamy breath merging above his head with the large clouds of misty vapour exuded by the Baskerville hounds.

"Wake up, young man.......come on. You went to bed early last night. Thought you'd be up before the birds this morning. Gaz is waiting downstairs to take you home," jollied Gramps while holding a tray of cherry and liquorice supreme biscuits for Olls' breakfast.

Olls was still curled up in his basket in a croissant shape trying to rub the sleep from his eyes.

"Oh and some fantastic news. I heard on Radio Dartmoor news this morning that the Baskerville hounds have been put in their place. Would you believe that we have a super dog hero in Devon? Apparently, challenged the hounds last night and scared them off the moor. Chap who works on the Baskerville farm reported it. They need some help and guidance, those beasts. Gone for special friendship training. Bullies they were. Never pays in the end." Gramps Bassett was chuckling to himself while leaning on his stick and reaching up with his other paw to open the curtains. "Means you'll be safe to get back on the moor with your Uncle next time you're down here."

Olls half raised his head from his basket.

"Like to meet the hero. Invite him round for tea. Treat him to one of my jus surprises," smiled Gramps.

Olls was now stretching from his basket and about to nibble a biscuit.

Gramps was just about to leave the room when he turned on his paws. "Having a tidy while you were sleeping this morning, young man, and put all that stuff from your Aunt Agatha's back in the bag. Strewn across the floor it was. Don't know what you want with it. Cloak, joke shop claws and fluorescent teeth. All full of bracken and mud, slime and I don't know what else. What do you young spaniels get up to? I don't know. Anyway, you hurry up now. Gaz'll have finished his tea and biscuits."

It was at least another twenty minutes before Olls had trotted downstairs, hugged and licked Gramps goodbye and was curled up on a bedding blanket in the back of Gaz's car.

"Well, my hooky, cooky friend. A good holiday? Any

24

adventures this time?" asked Gaz as he pressed the ignition.

"Not really, Gaz. Visited Aunt Agatha but wasn't allowed on the moor with Uncle Beage because of some dangerous dogs. But I ate plenty of Gramps Basset's liquorice jus. He's sent a large container of his favourite home with me for you and Helen to try. It's liquorice, fish paste, turnip, and mushroom flavoured," Said Olls, peering through the gap in the head rests but still looking sleepy.

"How thoughtful," grimaced Gaz. "Oh, well little fun then? In that case let's have a long game of snarl off when we get back home. Bet you will enjoy that, Olls."

"Just a bit out of practising with snarl off. Perhaps in a day or two," he yawned as he snuggled into the back seat and fell gently into the land of spaniel dreams.

Battle of the Bluebottle

P oodle Perm Pink, Wiggly Worm White, Bog Growlers' Grey, Barking Brown, Crusty Cat Cream, Rodent Rust, Orangutan Orange and eh.......well, that seems to be all up here, Ollie," said Mr Snipes turning his head away from the dusty top shelf and its paint pots before peering at the spaniel from the summit of his wooden steps.

"Hooky cooky," exclaimed Olls in disappointment while stretching from his back feet so that his front paws were high on to the shop counter. He could just about see over the top.

The ladder wobbled as Mr Snipes sighed then gingerly descended. His leather shoes had the appearance of cracked brown elephant hide and squeaked at every step which caused Olls' long scraggy ears to twitch.

"It just aint no good, Mr Snipes. I'll never get me kennel painted," panted Olls as he let go of the counter and sat looking up at the shopkeeper through brown eyes. He was fashion conscious and very particular when it came to choosing a paint colour for his home.

28

Mr Snipes turned from the bottom of his ladder, sniffed then looked down at the dog in a sad and apologetic way. As a remarkably thin but tall man he seemed lost inside his brown overall.

"There's always new-fangled paint colours coming in, Olls. Pop back in tomorrow." Mr Snipes' shiny beetle black hair sat firmly plastered to his head, yet occasionally he felt the need to run his fingers across its surface almost as if to check it was still there.

"Oh, go on have a biscuit. That'll cheer you up." Mr Snipes' hand left his hair and pulled out a small bone shaped biscuit from a paper bag under the counter.

Olls was disappointed but not so much that he had lost his appetite and could not crunch the treat or another if it were offered.

"Gaz says I have to make my kennel smart or there's no more holidays with Gramps Basset or riding Uncle Beage's motorbike. The old paint is peeling away," he said between biscuit crumb teeth.

"Well, I don't know why we have such fancy names for paint colours nowadays." A crumpled tissue was being nipped around Mr Snipes' shiny nose as he sniffed once more. Like Olls, the shopkeeper's nose was damp. But he didn't appear very healthy and raspberry red might have been an accurate way of describing it, he thought. "Different when I was a lad. Paints were simply paints. Ask your Aunt Agatha. She swore by plain black. What's wrong with a common red or blue or yellow or white? Anyway, have you thought about the brushes you'll need?"

But Olls wasn't really listening anymore. Instead he was turning towards the door with ears down, an aunt Agatha black look on his face and his tail between his legs.

Olls had only just pushed the door ajar with his snout when Mr Snipes called out urgently.

"Just wait a minute, my friend."

At the far side of the counter the shopkeeper was craned over a cardboard box like a heron fishing while running his bony fingers under some sticky tape.

"Looks like another delivery of paint. Yes.Oh, yes.... there's several tins: Whale Wheeze, Lizard Lime, Silver Seal, Panting Panther......and look at this, Olls," exclaimed Mr Snipes excitedly, "Dogs' Breath. Just what you've been waiting for. Cheer up. And if I am not mistaken I have a can of Lollipop Pink left in my stock room too for your inside."

Mr Snipes had barely lifted his bent back and mopped his runny nose with yet another tissue before the spaniel was rummaging through the box with his snout.

"Hooky cooky!"

"Thought you'd be pleased." Mr Snipes fingered a peppermint, which sat in a fluffy corner of his overall pocket with his tissues, before dropping it into his mouth.

Within moments he had appeared from behind a door with the Lollipop Pink and placed both cans of paint in a brown paper bag.

"Hooky cooky, Mr Snipes. Gaz is going to pay or Helen or something. Thanks, anyway….."

With the bag firmly gripped between his jaws Olls had disappeared leaving Mr Snipes calling after him in vain.

"You'll need brushes and brush cleaner and don't forget to rub down the peeling paint first!"

But all too late. The eager hound had disappeared into the side street leaving the door of 'Snipes' Paint Shop' jangling as it banged closed almost flattening the shopkeeper's nose.

Olls liked surprises and to surprise others too. In fact you were never quite certain what he might do next. His newly decorated kennel was to be a complete surprise to Gaz and Helen. They would return from work in the evening to be astonished by his artistic flair and painting skills. He might even be referred to as the Michelangelo of the canine world. Well, this is what he had hoped…

Both would stand back in astonishment and exclaim:

"Wow! Fantastic!"

"Amazing, spaniel!"

"You're a real professional."

"Love the colours."

"You deserve extra treats."

Olls adored treats, or 'tweats' as he called them, unless they were extra helpings of Gramps Bassett's liquorice and turnip jus.

There was no need to wait for help from Gaz and Helen as they had insisted. They were just humans and always busy. His father, Pop Ricks, was after all a pedigree field champion and like him, Olls believed, he had special skills. Which he had, of course but not as a painter and decorator.

He squeezed through his spaniel flap and into the house only just managing to drag the paint cans through with him. He was still panting after his run from the paint shop but there was no time to lose. There was work to be done.

Within moments he had set himself on the kitchen floor and prized open the paint lids with his claws. He nosed the wooden kennel to the middle of the room and was about to begin his wonderful work when a problem struck him. How was he to get the paint from the tin and onto the kennel? His paws were not going to be the answer to the problem as they were too big and had claws attached. What had Mr Snipes shouted at him so eagerly as he ran from his shop? Something about brushes?

Well, he had neither brushes nor time to return to Mr Snipes. For a few moments Olls sat looking at the paint pots and then at his kennel and then at his reflection in the window. It was his reflection that gave him the inspirational answer.

"Hooky cooky. That's the answer.....a brilliant idea." Olls was smiling and again pleased with himself. Like Pop Ricks he too was a champion of ideas. What he had seen mirrored in the window was a small, brush sized tail.

By using this as a guide Olls managed to manoeuvre his stumpy black tail into the can of Dogs' Breath right up to his bottom. As he lifted it globules of speckled paint dripped onto the tiled floor. By turning around and slapping his tail he could coat his flaky roof. This made his bottom itch and while not achieving the smoothest of finishes the paint was at least landing somewhere in the direction of his kennel.

"Hooky cooky," puffed Olls. Tricky work he thought but worth it. He stepped back to admire his progress. He had only applied three tail flicks of paint when something unexpectedly happened which signalled a change to the day.

At first Olls wasn't sure what was causing the irritating sound. Lifting his ears slightly, and twitching his eyebrows, he stopped painting. He twisted his head one way then another before cocking his head sideways. Before long

it became very clear to him. It was a buzzing and a dreadful droning that meant there was a menace in the room. A menace that caused him more irritation than anything else imaginable.

It was a BLUEBOTTLE FLY! A blue and green and black brute of a bluebottle.

To Olls, buzzing, hideous bluebottle flies were the worst enemy to any hound. "Hooky cooky. Kennel painting can wait a bit," he mumbled in a slightly growly way.

The monster was now clearly visible as it swooped like an enemy jet fighter plane. It had to be destroyed. Olls lifted his head towards the ceiling light as the metallic monster circled above him then darted and dived over the sink and towards the window. His eyes followed the insect's flight path.

Within seconds the spaniel had launched his initial attack. He leapt into the air streamlining his body into a missile, mouth open, jaws snapping until he bounced against the kitchen cupboards while the enemy, however, evaded his attack and continued its flight. But he was not going to be defeated by this giant fly. Olls shook his head and braced himself for a second charge. The fly was now spinning through the air and heading towards the fridge door. Without delay Olls leapt in determined pursuit.

Disaster struck immediately!

Despite a good deal more jaw snapping he missed the fly and landed instead with both rear paws in the paint pots. The force of his dive meant that he was now skidding and sliding across the tiled floor in paint pot skates at the speed of an Olympic athlete. Dogs Breath and Lollipop Pink coated his fur and splashed violently in huge waves across the entire kitchen.

Horror!

He only stopped after colliding with his kennel. Olls was now sitting in the middle of a muddy, vomit coloured paint sea with his head protruding through the kennel roof. It hung around him like a heavy necklace.

"Double hooky cooky."

There was neither sight nor sound of the bluebottle.

Olls must have been sitting silently in this mess for several minutes before he heard a knock on the back door.

"Can I come in, my friend?"

Fortunately, this was not the voice of either Gaz or Helen but one he nevertheless recognised as being friendly. The door slowly opened.

"Thought you might need a couple of decent brushes and some........." Mr Snipes' voice trailed away into amazed nothingness. He could not believe the picture before him. He sniffed and took another tissue from his pocket before blowing his nose.

"I've seen some of this new fancy modern art in galleries. Abstract I think they call it, Olls, but this is a quite an unbelievable mess. I wondered what Dogs' Breath might look like out of the can. Interesting to say the least. Here, let me help you out of that kennel."

Mr Snipes stepped over pools of liquid in his squeaky shoes as best he could and helped the spaniel up, carefully removing his paint pot skates and the kennel necklace.

Amazingly, Olls had suffered nothing more serious than a bruise or two. However, the kitchen resembled a battlefield.

"I think we both have a few hours hard work ahead of this afternoon, Olls," slurped Mr Snipes while sucking a peppermint, "and it's already midday."

"Hello, my boy. Have you been good today?" Helen was first into the kitchen at 6'oclock that afternoon. She dropped her bag onto the table and bent down to pat Olls' head. "Well, it certainly looks tidier and cleaner in the kitchen than when I left you with the breakfast pots morning."

"Very much tidier," agreed Gaz in surprise.

Olls sat sheepishly in his bed and looked up while wagging his tail and keeping his paws crossed. He tried desperately to look innocent of any wrong doing.

"Mmmnn.......there's something different, though. Where's that old kennel gone that you were going to paint?"

"You see, Mr Snipes came round today and he said......."

"Said what, Olls?" Questioned Gaz suspiciously.

Olls was feeling nervous and exhausted and looked at the floor as he spoke. "He said that the kennel was too scruffy to paint and he had ordered a new one for me from 'Dogs R Us' and the new wood would need to be painted..... and hooky, cooky and......"

"It was very kind of him to take the old one away and order a brand new one and even help you tidy the kitchen while he was here," commented Helen as she removed her coat.

"A real friend you have there, Olls," remarked Gaz. " I think we should call round to thank him at the weekend and buy some paint for the new kennel. We can help you, remember. Nothing fancy, let's just keep to a simple red or blue or yellow, shall we?"

The spaniel's eyes remained fixed to the floor as he nodded in agreement.

Helen crouched down to Olls once more and ruffled his curly ears. "A busy day, by the sound of things and you're probably too tired for a game of snarl off in the garden with Gaz." She paused. "But somehow you have managed to get some flakes of paint into your ears and tail. Awful mucky colour too. Who would ever have used paint like that?"

"Hooky cooky," sighed Olls with his head between his paws. "No idea. A real mystery, Helen."

Martian Marny

"Let me introduce meself, cousin. I'm Marny and tings are goin' to change round here for a while, yer podgy working class spaniel."

Marny prodded Olls in the chest with a rock hard paw and hissed his words with menace. Olls gasped for breath and looked worried.

"I'm a working cocker spaniel not working class," corrected Olls. "My pop Ricks had a pedigree and I've got a certificate."

"Yer what I say you is," ordered the Martian dog in his New York gangster voice.

Olls had been trapped inside the garden shed and pinned against the wall unable to move. Terracotta flower pots, a rake, spades and bamboo canes surrounded him as Marny barred his exit to the door.

"Now, I tink we're goin' to start wid some of those treats or tweats as we both like to call them. Hand 'em over, cousin."

Olls dropped a small bag from his paws. The paper

44

split on contact with the floor. Without hesitation, Marny's snout followed the contents as they scattered everywhere before he gobbled the bone shaped biscuits instantly. Olls could only look on as a spectator as Marny raised his head, licked his lips and pushed him against the garden canes. Martian breath smelt of sour milk, rotten cheese and steamed brussel sprouts.

"That'll do for starters. I'm pullin' the shots now. Less of da walks and cosy nights by da fire for you, cus. It's my turn for some luxury."

Olls gulped and felt helpless.

"And what's wid da perfume?" Marny craned his neck towards Olls and twitched his nose as he sniffed. "Been to that poodle parlour for pampered pooches again? Paw waxing, blueberry facials and butter milk baths, eh?"

Olls gulped for a second time.

"Anyway, I'll be back," snarled Marny. "I'll be back. In the meantime take it easy in here." With that he grabbed Olls by his red collar and pushed him to the floor before slinking away and slamming the shed door behind him. The sound of its cold clicking into a locked position horrified Olls.

In appearance Marny could be mistaken for Ollie. Well, that is when Olls had just returned from a rather enthusiastic and scissor happy barber at the 'Grooming

Parlour'. Marny clearly was a dog of sorts. He was of spaniel proportions with spaniel ears and wore the same red collar but he was unlike Olls in any other way.

A dog head pushed open the door which divided the garden from the kitchen. Marny licked Olls' food bowl then vacuumed the kitchen floor with his black whiskered snout in the hope of finding toast or biscuit crumbs. Next he jumped onto the work surfaces and sniffed for anything edible.

Disappointed by his lack of success he leapt straight onto a kitchen chair and sat bolt upright as if waiting to be served at a posh restaurant.

"What are you doing up there Olls?" grumbled Helen as she swept into the kitchen. "Down at once."

Marny fixed her with a disobedient stare. There was a pause followed by a few seconds of silence while the dog refused to move.

"I said down from that chair, please. Whatever's got into you today?"

Reluctantly, the dog jumped back to the floor muttering his disapproval.

"You've had a short cut at the grooming parlour today. Not sure that I like it quite as tight as that. Hardly recognise you, Olls." Helen ran both her hands down his back. "Still you won't need another soon, I suppose."

"Have me fur how I likes it. My rules. About time you fed me, aint it? Come on, come on," he mumbled through his teeth. "Time for tweats......"

"Gaz will feed you when he cooks, soon." Helen said sternly and left the kitchen.

Marny mooched around the kitchen impatiently putting his paws up on work surfaces and sniffing and snorting for any crumbs of food. When it came time for feeding he pushed Gaz away from his bowl before he had time to finish filling it and gulped the spaniel nuts in seconds

A little later that evening Gaz and Helen sat at the kitchen table as usual for dinner looking slightly concerned.

"I don't know what's got into Ollie," Helen said through mouthfuls of seafood pasta. "He just isn't himself. He seems so rude and disobedient."

Gaz nodded steadily in agreement.

"Somehow he even looks different. I know he's had a very short cut but still just not our Ollie."

"Maybe he's ill," said Helen sadly. "Maybe I should take him to the vet in the morning just to check."

"Perhaps.....and I know that Olls has had a slight New York accent since that episode with the language learning course but.......well, I mean his accent seems so much more pronounced today," puzzled Gaz.

He finished his last mouthful and put the cutlery onto his plate. "I suppose it could just be that he's exhausted after his holiday with Grandpa Basset. He spent so much time riding over the moors with Uncle Beage on that oily motor bike. And, of course, there were those visits to Aunt Agatha while he was down there. He doesn't enjoy those and finds them 'boring', as he says."

"It's possible, I suppose. And I think the kennel painting episode took it out of him. But I'm just not sure..............."

The only sounds to be heard over the next few minutes were clatters and clinks as the pots and pans and cutlery from the evening meal were gathered and placed into the sink for washing. Suddenly, however, the calm was broken by ear splitting sounds bursting from the sitting room.

Instantly, Gaz dropped his tea towel on the floor and raced into the next room. His ears were met by the howling and growling of a very excited dog and a booming television set. His eyes could not believe their sight. Marny was standing on the sofa caught between chewing the cushions and yelping at the screen. His ears were horizontal from his head as he bounced up and down as if he was on a trampoline.

Scattered around him, and all over the carpet, were half eaten dog chew treats and goose feathers.

49

50

"What the......?!"

Gaz had no chance to finish as he was interrupted by Marny.

"Ha, move it, Gaz. Yer blocking da screen. 'Dangerous Dogs'. What a film! Just da best. Ever seen it? Stars Royston Rottweiler and the Bull Dog Bunch......"

Momentarily, Gaz was speechless before grabbing the remote control and switching the set off. "I have not seen it and I don't think I ever want to. Get down now and get to your basket," he said pointing towards the kitchen.

"Cool it, Gaz. What's got into yer? Can't a dog have a bit of fun round here?"

"TO YOUR BASKET!"

"Ok....ok......spoil me fun if you 'ave to."

Marny hopped from the sofa and sloped off towards the kitchen and Ollie's basket, his ears hanging in a vertical position once more.

Standing by the sitting room door Helen looked in amazement at the debris.

"Told you he's ill. To the vets in the morning, I think," muttered Helen shaking her head and reaching for the vacuum cleaner.

Upstairs Gaz and Helen slept peacefully that night unaware of the whimpering and scratching inside the garden shed. Ollie was now hungry and thirsty. He had eaten nothing since the morning, other than a few fragments of biscuit crumb, and was surviving on stale and gritty brown water from a flower pot. He was desperate to escape but eventually dropped to the floor and onto a rough piece of sacking in exhaustion. Through the darkness, meanwhile, Marny stalked the kitchen growling and mumbling to himself. Occasionally, he would stop to rip the corners of Ollie's bed and spit the woolly padding onto the floor.

"He hasn't recovered," said Gaz disappointedly next morning. He handed Helen a cup of tea as she sat up in bed rubbing her morning eyes.

"Really is alien behaviour. Looks as if it's been snowing in the kitchen. He's chewed the wadding from his bed and scattered it everywhere. Shredded his toy fox too! I'll just finish my tea then take him for a run in the church field. See if that helps. At least he'll be out of the house. Guess you best take him to the vets then if he's no better."

Helen put her tea mug on the bedside table and reached for her mobile phone. "I'll ring Mr Hawkins at the surgery now."

The church field dew sparkled in sunlight and the morning was alive with birdsong chatter and walkers and dogs of all shapes and sizes. Perfection.

Well, it began as a perfect morning walk. Marny was soon let loose from his lead and ran sniffing and wagging his tail in the hedgerows.

"Good morning," called Gaz to a familiar faced dog walker.

"It's a beautiful day," the fellow dog walker replied cheerfully and raised a hand in friendly acknowledgment. "Ollie must be loving his run."

"I'm sure," agreed Gaz.

Gaz turned away to face the direction in which Marny had run moments earlier but there was no sign of him anywhere.

"Ollie...Ollieeee!" called Gaz proceeded by a shrill whistle through his teeth.

Nothing.

Slowly, Gaz turned a full circle continuing to whistle and call while shielding his eyes from the sunlight.

Still no response.

A few moments of silent panic were replaced by sudden cries from the far corner of the field. "Come here, you! Give it back now. It's not yours!"

54

An angry looking man was hopelessly chasing a black spaniel. He ran in ever increasing circles in pursuit of the dog who had clearly stolen his young daughter's doll. Despite desperate lunges at the dog his efforts were in vain. Instead the spaniel alternately dropped the doll then growled and barked at the girl in the pushchair who was screaming in terror.

This was horrendous. Frantically, Gaz started running towards the scene.

"Ollie, come here. Drop it! Drop it! Now!"

But the situation worsened. The bald headed, chubby father had slowed in his pursuit and was bent double with his hands on his knees panting and wheezing while the dog sat and chewed the legs of the plastic doll as if to taunt them both. Next, the spaniel lifted his back leg over the push chair for a few seconds before running towards the wood leaving a disgusting yellow liquid dripping from the wheels and onto the grass.

"Is that your dog?" bellowed the figure now standing upright and holding his lower back with both hands.

"I think it might be," suggested Gaz in embarrassment, trying to catch his breath also while standing in the middle of chewed plastic doll limbs.

"It's a disgrace. Can't you control it? My daughter's in terrible shock. Snarling and showing her its ugly teeth. What you going to do about it?" The father's shiny cheeks had reddened into tomato blobs.

His daughter's yelling subsided to a constant snivel. She rubbed snotty hands into her blond curly hair as the man bent down to wipe her eyes and nose with a tissue he had found in his pocket.

"Dogs need training. He's vicious and shouldn't be allowed off the lead. What have you got to say for yourself?"

"Well, he's never behaved like this before and well..... he may be ill and......." All Gaz's explanations seemed feeble.

The man had returned to a gentler pink complexion now but still looked annoyed as he listened in silence with his arms crossed in front of his chest.

The dog had completely disappeared.

Several minutes of humble apology followed with an offer from Gaz to replace the doll and clean the pushchair and take Ollie to training school, should he ever be found.

Before long ,Gaz was walking back through the field towards home with a dogless lead hanging beside him. All he could do was relay the morning's dreadful episode to Helen and report a missing dog to the police. He felt disappointed, saddened and a little angry and wondered why Ollie had become so disobedient and poorly behaved.

He took a deep breath as he entered the house dreading the prospect of describing the morning's events but to his surprise was met by a smile from Helen and a rather dishevelled black spaniel by her side.

"How long has he been here?" There was a brief pause. "You'll never guess what he's done," Gaz said pointing accusingly at Ollie. "Oh, the shame and embarrassment. Wait until tell you. You won't believe it."

"I think I had better tell you Ollie's story first. That might explain most of it. Let's go into the kitchen for a cup of tea first."

After half an hour and two cups of tea later they were both slumped into kitchen chairs with Ollie sitting upright at the table, chewing a tweat and nodding in agreement with everything Helen had said. She finished the explanation by saying, "Well, I only found him because I went into the garden shed to look for the terracotta pots for planting and there he was shivering on an old sack."

"Extraordinary......Well, let me phone the police. There's still a poorly behaved dog on the loose somewhere," said Gaz patting Olls on the head.

He turned back towards Helen and Olls then hesitated before picking up the phone." What's all this about a Martian dog, though? A cousin? It's crazy. Just nonsense."

By lunch time the mood in the house had calmed to somewhere near normality when Helen said, "Put the radio on. I've not heard the news today."

Gaz switched on the set above the fridge just in time to hear studio laughter from the end of a comedy quiz followed by the headlines.

"These are the news headlines this Saturday lunchtime," said the stern voiced presenter. "There are several reports coming in from across the country that gangs of gangster dogs, claiming to be from Mars, are invading homes and bullying domestic pets and their families. Some dogs are posing as relatives.

"Police have advised all pet owners to be aware of the danger and report any incidents or sightings immediately. Battersea Dog Home has spoken of riots and some break outs while a few children have claimed that small craft from outer space have been landing in parks and playgrounds with sounds of yelping, cheering and barking coming from inside. We hope to have an update for listeners later."

Olls slept comfortably later that night but before drifting into a blissful sleep he looked up from his patched and repaired bed and stared through the window towards the night sky. A myriad of stars, planets and possibly silver spaceships glowed in the purply darkness.

"Hooky cooky. All a bit strange," he yawned. "Don't know where Marny came from or where he's gone or what made him such a bully but I'm glad to have my bed back."

Vinyl Talking
(When R becomes W)

One evening when Olls was little more than a black bundle of a puppy Helen came home with an excited tone to her voice.

"You'll never guess what I found today, Olls," she said as she swept into the kitchen opening a shopping bag.

A bone or a carrot or biscuit treat, Olls would have hoped. But it was none of these.

"Look at this. I found it in a charity shop next to Mr Snipes' Paint Shop," she said.

Out of her bag came a square cardboard sleeve from which she slid a circular but flat piece of plastic. It was as black and shiny as Grandpa Basset's liquorice nose and the size of a dinner plate. Maybe it's something to keep my teeth clean and my breath fresh, Olls thought. The front of the sleeve was covered in drawings of huge skyscrapers and a tall statue of a grand figure holding aloft a flaming torch. Across the middle of the cover in very large bubbly print it read, 'Teach Yourself English the Easy Way.'

"This is just what you need to help you understand English, you know human words and begin talking," she said placing the plastic on the chair.

He wasn't quite sure what she meant but it was too large to eat or chew. Perhaps you just licked and sucked it instead like an enormous liquorice lollipop.

Within a few moments Helen had rushed out of the room leaving Olls to sniff the plastic and wag his tail before returning almost immediately with a wooden box which she placed on the table. Alongside this she arranged a pair of large headphones which were then connected to it. There was a picture of a small white dog on the box who was clearly listening with interest to sounds coming from a horn.

"Come on, jump up," she said while patting a chair by the table. Suspiciously but curiously Olls leapt onto the seat. Helen opened the lid to the box and placed the disc onto a circular rotating pad and a plastic arm onto the disc. Soon it was spinning round and round very quickly and was making Olls feel dizzy to watch. The headphones were stretched over his ears. He couldn't hear Helen now just a voice speaking to him from inside the headphones, a type of voice which he hadn't heard before.

"This is how my parents listened to music long before the invention of CDs, mobile phones and all today's tricky technical stuff. Luckily, I kept their old gramophone in the garage," she said. "Wouldn't it

be nice if you could speak a few words, Olls, a little English?"

Olls couldn't understand much in his early pup days but could make out some things by the tone of her voice and the look on her face. Words like 'walk', 'biscuit', 'treats' and 'Ollie dinner' were important and seemed well worth remembering.

"Wouldn't it be nice if we could chat about the weather or the news or your favourite smells?" she said.

The dog looked up at her with his head cocked slightly to one side, listening to the words from the headphones but understanding little and unable to answer. He just kept focussing on a man's voice and watching Helen's lips move despite the fact he could not hear her.

"Wouldn't it be nice if we could talk about fashion, food and walks and chasing balls in the park?" she said with a smile, leaning towards Olls while cocking her head too.

"Wouldn't it be nice if........?" And so she went on unheard by the spaniel who now stared through the window at the pigeons balancing on the fence while another voice blabbered into his ears.

For several days after this Olls was beckoned onto a chair in the kitchen with the promise of a biscuit treat and had the headphones fixed over his shaggy ears. He was not always keen to learn and would have preferred to be outside chasing the pigeons, sniffing the bushes, chewing grass and running through the fields.

"Time to listen to some more of the 'Teach Yourself English Course," Helen would say gleefully. Alongside the box she now placed a pack of picture cards which she turned over each time Olls looked up at her. She knew then the voice had said something fresh to teach the dog.

"I'm sure you'll pick up some words very soon now. Here, have another biscuit." Olls leaned over and snuffled the crumbly treat from her outstretched palm.

The man's voice was certainly strange and not of an accent which he had heard before. He sounded nothing like Gaz or Mr Snipes or any other man he had met. Olls continued to listen to the voice, fixing his eyes on the cards each time Helen turned the next one over. There were pictures of buildings, vehicles, animals, insects, bottles, food, and humans in costumes and many things which Olls had never seen before in his life. Occasionally, there would be songs and poems too.

The spaniel continued to listen and watch as Helen encouraged him. Very occasionally his lips curled around his teeth as he clearly tried to imitate the words and grumbly growly sounds spluttered from his throat.

"Where's Ollie?' called Gaz entering the kitchen and loosening his tie.

It was a gloriously warm late Friday afternoon several weeks after the first language lesson when Gaz and Helen returned to the house from a busy week at work.

"Mmnnn......he's not up here," responded Helen in reply from the top of the stairs.

There were a few brief moments of concern for the spaniel's whereabouts before Gaz shouted, "Quickly, down here. Look at this in the garden!"

Helen hurried down to join Gaz in the kitchen.

"Just look and listen," said Gaz in astonishment.

They both moved close to the kitchen window which overlooked the garden. Afternoon shadows folded themselves over the bottom half of the lawn while sunlight spotlighted the top where a performance of sorts was about to start. Two pigeons perched in the gallery on the highest branches of the cherry tree while a curious tabby cat looked on from the safety of the garden wall.

In astonishment Gaz said, "Can you believe it?" He edged closer to the window for a better look.

Helen was apparently too dumbfounded to answer but followed.

An approving chorus of barks and yelps followed almost instantly and a troupe of mottled mongrels with tatty ears performed back flips while the pigeons flew form the branches and swooped across the stage before returning to the tree. A crescent shaped audience of local dogs had gathered for this matinee performance. Some like Pup Spugs, Cornish Flossie and her Sprocker friends Chester and Toby, Pansy Poodle, Ronnie Rottweiler and Tinker Toby were all known friends but other dogs had gathered that hadn't been seen before. The terrier, Sergeant Shaun had positioned himself on the shoulders of Shirty Bertie and Jack spaniel for a prime view.

"This aftewnoon I will pewfowm with songs, poems and much more. To show appweciation please feel fwee to drop doggy tweats, bones and discarded toast cwusts into my bowl as you leave."

Gaz and Helen continued to look on through the window too astonished to move or say anything.

"Fwiends, womans and countwymen lend me your ears." Jack Spaniel howled to the sky in excitement as Olls began to recite lines from Shakespeare.

"A wose would smell as sweet....."

Olls' performance continued breathlessly for at least an hour. He dipped into lines from famous old films, including 101 Dalmatians, and finished by singing, 'How Much is that Doggy in the Window' in front of his tail wagging audience. The entire show was only interrupted by a brief toilet break and a ball chasing game through the flower beds instigated by Olls himself.

By the time Olls had finished, and every dog satisfied had gone, shadows engulfed the entire garden. The cat had slinked away to his own backyard soon after the rendition of 'Three Blind Mice.' Contentedly the pigeons slept.

Gaz and Helen had made a cup of tea before the encore and were sitting at the kitchen table still too amazed by what they had witnessed to say much when Olls strolled through the back door looking weary and breathless.

"What can I say, Olls?" sighed Helen after a brief pause. "You clearly have been listening very hard to your language course and we can chat together from now but I wish you hadn't invited so many friends though. It will take all evening to clear up the garden and rescue my battered geraniums."

"Pity your audience didn't leave you many treats. The pigeons have eaten the crusts or should I say cwusts," remarked Gaz with a smile as he picked up Olls' bowl which rattled with a solitary dog biscuit. "You've earned a good dinner tonight though."

"I aint pewfect, yet but me talking is getter gooder, aint it?" Said Olls looking up from tired brown eyes.

Within a few minutes the contented spaniel had licked his bowl clean after a full dinner and was curled up and snoozing in his basket close to the boiler. Occasionally, he could be heard muttering words and phrases in his sleep presumably learned from his course.

"Put up yer hands bud this is a bank waid," Olls whimpered at one moment before snoring again.

During this Gaz was preparing dinner by the cooker when he turned to Helen and said in a puzzled tone, "You know Olls is impressive. He's only been learning for a few weeks and his grammar needs working on but more than that he sounds like an American gangster. Have you noticed that often he seems to pronounce his R as W?"

"Yeh, I had thought that too. He's staying with Grandpa Basset next week. Not sure what he and Uncle Beage will make of it all."

"Pass me the vinyl record sleeve would you?" said Gaz putting a saucepan on the stove.

After examining the front cover for a moment he turned it over and began reading the information on the back for clues. Before long something was dawning on his face. Something was becoming clearer.

"I think I know why this was in the charity shop sale. Just look at what it says in the notes on the back."

Eagerly Helen reached for the record cover and started to read aloud some of the print. Suddenly she stopped and looked up with an incredulous expression on her face. "Oh, no! That explains it. 'Teach yourself English in ten easy lessons. The New York version in gangster style.'"

"Well that's going to take some changing now," commented Gaz.

70

"Probably," agreed Helen, "but we'll have to try. His Aunt Agatha is very particular about language being spoken correctly."

Just then Olls broke from his snoring with another American whimper in his sleep. "Stop messing wid me bud and wun. You're a wascal!"

"Yes, looks like quite a big task ahead," agreed Helen holding her hands to her head.

Printed in Great Britain
by Amazon